THE
GLASS
OF
LEAD&GOLD

CORNELIA FUNKE

THE
GLASS
OF
LEAD & GOLD

with illustrations by the author

PUSHKIN CHILDREN'S

Pushkin Press
71–75 Shelton Street
London WC2H 9JQ

First published by Pushkin Press in 2018
This edition first published in 2019

1 3 5 7 9 8 6 4 2

ISBN 13: 978-1-78269-209-6

Designed and typeset by Tetragon, London
Printed and bound by CPI Group (UK) Ltd, Croydon CR0 4YY

www.pushkinpress.com

THE
GLASS
OF
LEAD & GOLD

For
Keith John Mastrorocco
who inspired this story

I T HAD BEEN SNOWING ALL NIGHT, the flakes swirling down on Londra as if the stars were falling from the sky to make the city shine for Christmas Eve. The snow had covered the cobblestoned streets with so thick a blanket that it hushed all the sounds the city made while waking, and its softness made Tabetha nearly forget how cold it felt beneath her worn-out shoes. The narrow alleys she took to get to the river bank were the same as every day, but today the grimy houses lining them looked like they belonged in a baker's window: the roofs covered with icing, the chimneys puffing powdered sugar into the slowly paling sky. For a moment, Tabetha could almost believe that as the snow melted it would take away all the ugliness and sadness underneath. Maybe then, Londra would emerge as the shiny, magical place Tabetha's mother had told her about every night, when they'd still lived in the village by the sea.

Tabetha barely thought about it these days—the draughty cottages by the shores of a grey sea, the nets she had helped her father to repair, the fish drawing their last breath on the planks of his boat, along with starfish and tiny seahorses—all that seemed as unreal as the snow-covered houses surrounding her. Her father had drowned shortly after her seventh birthday, and her mother had packed their bags to begin a new life in Londra, the faraway city filled with laughter and light she had told Tabetha about. They found out, quite soon, however, that the light and laughter came at a price only the rich could afford.

Her mother had died two years after their arrival in the city. She had become little more than one of the stories she had loved to tell—fairy tales too beautiful to believe in, amid all the poverty and darkness her daughter had experienced ever since. It was not easy to survive alone in Londra, but in three days' time, Tabetha Brown would celebrate her fifteenth birthday. She'd promised herself a small piece of cake to celebrate the occasion, though she had yet to earn the money to afford such luxury.

Getting older made life easier. In her first years alone, Tabetha had often been so hungry that she'd been tempted to make her way back to the village — but then she'd remember her grandfather yelling at her or her mother, and how often she'd felt the slaps of his rough hands on her face, or his stick on her back. No. Life was hard everywhere, and Londra was her home now.

She picked up a stone and chased a bony cat away from a small figure stretched out in the snow. It was a Hob, his thin arms and legs as stiff as sticks. Londra's population of tiny men and women was almost as numerous as its mice and rats, both in the poor and rich quarters of the city. Hobs didn't get much bigger than a crow, and could be quite grumpy, but they were hard workers. In return for their services, they usually only asked for an old shirt or coat,

11

to tailor their own clothes from, some food to feed their families—which, admittedly could be quite big—and for lodgings under a stair or closet. They worked in restaurants and factories and in the big mansions on the other side of the city, but they did not always receive the gratitude they deserved and, especially in winter, one found many of them dead in the streets.

This one was still breathing though and Tabetha leant the tiny creature against a shop window, hoping the warmth seeping through the glass might bring him back to life. Soon

after her mother's death, she'd ended up working for a chimney sweep who'd made her climb up so many chimneys that her skinny legs were soon covered with soot and scars. She'd been sure she'd end up like so many children working for the sweeps, who slipped and broke their necks—until a family of Hobs helped her escape. She had never forgotten that kindness.

The sweep had never realized she was a girl. It was hard for anyone to survive in Londra, but almost impossible for a woman— the hardship of her mother's life had been proof of that—so Tabetha kept her hair short, and dressed like a boy. At first, she'd missed her long hair and dresses, but now she preferred the pants and shirts she wore—though she had to add more and more layers of rags to hide her growing breasts.

Fifteen… No, life wouldn't get easier.

Before she reached the steep stairs leading down to the muddy shore of the Themse, she found three more Hobs and, right next to the steps, a coin shimmering in the snow like an early Christmas gift. It was a good beginning to a day that usually made her feel sad. Maybe she'd finally even be able to buy a pair of old shoes from the Leprechaun who lived under the stairs of the theatre, in whose draughty backyard she found shelter during the night.

There were already two-dozen mudlarks out on this early Christmas Eve morning, searching the frozen mud of the river bank for copper wire, old coins, metals and other sellable goods. Tabetha knew them all. Most of the others were older than her. Mudlarking was not a healthy business. The filth-ridden mud often reached up to their knees and any small wound could cause lethal infection.

Then there were the tides. Tabetha had watched with her own eyes how the rising waters had swept away an old woman and her son. But the river bank was a dangerous place—even on a day like this, when the tide was low and the mud was frozen—for it was the hunting ground of Watermen and Kelpies, not to mention drunken sailors, Elven-dust dealers and smugglers of all kinds.

None of the other mudlarks suspected that Ted, as Tabetha usually introduced herself, was a girl. She stayed away from them anyway, as she was sure each of them would steal from her if she gave them the opportunity. Nobody could be trusted. Nobody. She had only survived because she never forgot that.

When Tabetha reached the end of the stairs, she spotted an unfamiliar figure: a stout, balding man, far too well-dressed for a mudlark. He was handing Limpey some kind of paper. Maybe he was a preacher, who'd come to convince them to go to church tomorrow for Christmas. Some of the others would follow such an invitation for sure, as they were all very talented pickpockets. Tabetha had tried that trade, too, but it had made her feel ashamed, whereas discovering things in the river mud filled her with pride. The objects she found were all lost and broken, like she was, but they'd survived the river, they'd come a long way, and they each had their own story to tell.

None of the other mudlarks had Tabetha's patience when it came to scanning the river bank, or her sharp eyes when it came to spotting treasure in the mud and debris the huge river brought back from distant seas and washed up from long-forgotten times. Tabetha was not sure whether she loved or hated the Themse. At times, its shores felt like her only home, but on days like these — when other people sat in their houses, surrounded by their families — the wide ever-moving waters made her feel even more homeless.

Stop it! she told herself. Self-pity was the poison she feared most. It fed on your heart. Most of the time, they all waded through the poisonous mud barefoot, with their trousers rolled up, but today the cold meant the mudlarks kept their leaking boots on.

The small piece of torn rope Tabetha spotted after just a few steps was a good example of the treasure the others so easily missed. She made sure her face expressed only boredom while she bent down, to make sure she didn't give away that she'd found something of value. A few shimmering scales clung to the rope;

Mermaid scales. The river had carried them all the way from the southern coast, where Tabetha had seen them so often on the beach near her village.

Mermaid scales were very sought after by tailors, who embroidered the robes of their rich clients with them. She was just carefully slipping her find into one of the leather pouches she'd tied to the old belt the river had brought her, when she saw that the well-dressed stranger she'd spotted from the stairs was watching her. He looked strong and fast, despite his age — always an important consideration, in case one had to run — but none of the others seemed worried. His coat was not as well-tailored as that of the banker who had his coachman stop by the stairs every Sunday, after church, to throw a few handfuls of pennies down — but the man's boots certainly cost more than her findings would earn her in ten years, and the scarf around his stout neck at least three. What was his profession? Tabetha could usually guess, but not in this case.

"I hear you're one of the best mudlarks on the river."

His accent was New Caledonian. Tabetha's grandfather came from up north. As for the compliment — it was definitely made up, to flatter her. None of the other mudlarks would ever admit she was better than most of them.

The man had a scar on his forehead and another one on his hand, but he didn't look like a soldier or professional fighter, and no policeman could afford those boots. A Thumbling peeked out of his coat pocket, its pale, amber eyes scanning Tabetha's pockets and pouches. Thumblings were the most gifted thieves, and although they were barely bigger than a gin bottle, not even the most fast-fingered human could compete with them.

"Don't worry. He steals only when I tell him to."

The stranger smiled, his thin lips revealing three silver teeth. Tabetha tried hard not to stare at them. They were marked with some kind of ancient lettering.

"Have you ever found a piece of glass that looked like it could be part of this?"

The bit of paper he produced from his pocket was a clipping from a newspaper. When he handed it to her, she noticed that the skin on his left hand was covered with burn marks and two of his fingernails were missing. He clearly had a dangerous profession.

There was an illustration on the clipping, one of those black and white etchings she loved to look at. Tabetha couldn't read, but those images allowed her to learn about the world nevertheless and she picked up every newspaper she found on the street, just to look at them. This one was quite boring though, compared to the ones showing battles or faraway cities. It showed only a glass with a slender stem and delicate engravings of Sand Fairies and Fire Elves.

"No one will find this, mister," she said. "Thin glass like that has no chance of surviving the river."

Glass, porcelain, burnt clay... The mud of the Themse was spiked with millions of shards from mugs, bottles and plates, and it took a very skilled eye to detect whether they had any value. Most of them didn't, but the older ones sometimes got you some money from the collectors on Celt Street, who were obsessed with everything ancient. Tabetha loved the stories they told when she brought them something they got excited about: stories about old kings and knights, enchanted swords, Fairies whom princes killed themselves for or child-eating Witches. She had found quite a few of the small pots the Witches sold their potions in. They were almost as common as the clay pipes men used to smoke Elven dust in. The pipes with bowls shaped like faces brought good money.

"What's so special about that glass?" Tabetha said, handing the newspaper clipping back to the stranger.

"Keep it." He gave her another silver-toothed smile. "The glass only has sentimental value, but I will pay three silver shillings if you find me a fragment."

Sentimental value? They all thought it was so easy to sell lies to children. But three silver shillings… It was more than she earned in ten good months, even if she searched the mud for sixteen hours a day.

"You can find me at the Red Lion. You know where that pub is?"

Tabetha nodded. It was a place for rich people who liked to pretend they were less well-off than they were.

"Ask for Bartholomew Jakes." The Thumbling still had his eyes on her pouches. "But if you don't find a piece of that glass before the end of Christmas Day, don't bother. I need it by tomorrow night, and I am not interested in old coins or whatever else you usually sell."

He gave her a nod, plucked a seagull feather off his well-tailored sleeve and walked back to the stairs, in his fine boots.

Tabetha looked at the image in her hand, and glanced over to the others. No-teeth Harry, Limpey, Frogeater… They all held a clipping, and they returned her glance with the same fierce frown she gave them. Tabetha had been friends with another mudlark only once. Midget. A Waterman had killed him, when he went after a wooden crate floating by on the dirty waves. She hadn't been able to go near the river for more than a week after that. It is hard to lose a friend, especially when you have only one.

It began to snow again. The river swallowed the flakes like a huge, wet, grey-skinned beast, and Tabetha searched the cold mud until the sun set, veiled in chimney smoke, and the waters of the Themse turned as black as the boots the scarred stranger had worn. She found some copper wire, a tin spoon and a few coins, of which she suspected one to be quite old. Along with the Mermaid scales, it wasn't too bad a harvest, but as always, she made sure she looked disappointed when she headed for the stairs.

The river bank was even more dangerous at night, and even the boldest mud-larks left with the last light of day. Tabetha was sure they'd all searched for the glass, but of course none of them would have given away their success by leaving suspiciously early or — as a boy called Oyster had once foolishly done — by climbing up the stairs smiling and whistling. No-teeth Harry and Limpey had stolen the golden ring he had found the same night, after beating him up.

No. There were no smiles when they headed up the stairs. They all wore their mudlark faces, expressionless and smeared with river mud. "We should turn ourselves into Goyl, Ted," Midget had once teased her. "All stone, with fire in our eyes."

Neither of them had ever seen a Goyl. Goyl lived on the continent and hated to cross open water, so they rarely made it to Albion, but everyone had heard about them. They were the stone-skinned siblings of man: golden eyed and at home underground, where they built cities from precious stone. Tabetha imagined them to look like the statues in front of the Queen's palace, staring down from their pedestals with empty marble eyes.

There were rumours that the Goyl king had beaten the Albion fleet, and that they built flying machines and could turn humans into Goyl just by scratching your skin with their claws. But those were only tales to scare children. Midget had sometimes pretended he was a Goyl, chasing her down the river bank, clawing the cold, wet air with his dirty fingers. Curse that Waterman. She really missed Midget. Sometimes she dreamt of the Waterman dragging her down too, all the way down to the bottom of the river, to keep her prisoner amongst his piles of golden treasure—people said that's what they did with girls.

The snow made it easier than usual to wash the stench of the mud off their hands. The others hastily headed home to whatever wretched place they found shelter at for the night, but Tabetha decided to stop at an inn first, one which overlooked the river and was mostly frequented by sailors and dock workers: the Fuentes' Soup Kitchen. Tabetha couldn't read the name, but the metal sign above the door—shaped like a seal with a woman's head—had always stirred her curiosity, and only a few months ago the cold had finally drawn her through the narrow door, into the smoke-filled room behind it with its handful of wooden tables.

The smells that welcomed her when she opened the door on this Christmas Eve were so delicious they made her empty stomach hurt.

The girl who was arguing with a drunken guest at the counter was probably not much older than Tabetha, though in the red dress she wore she looked grown up. The pearls in her chestnut hair proved to be Will-o'-the-Wisps and Grass Elves when Tabetha came closer, but the lipstick and the soot-lined eyebrows were definitely real. Her name was Ofelia, as far as Tabetha remembered, and she was the oldest daughter of the owners and usually served at the tables or helped with the dirty dishes.

Tabetha had come looking for Ofelia's mother, but she couldn't see her anywhere. The Fuentes had opened the Soup Kitchen just a year ago. Rumour had it they employed a Troll woman as their cook, who had killed three men in her home country before she had come to Londra, because they hadn't appreciated her cooking. Everyone knew that Trolls were very touchy, and deadly when they were angry, but as Tabetha had never set foot in the Fuentes' kitchen, she wasn't sure whether to believe the story. Some of the other mudlarks also swore that Ofelia Fuentes's mother was a Witch, but they said that about almost every woman, especially the ones who managed to make a living for themselves.

Alfonso Fuentes, Ofelia's father, was said to be one of the main gardeners at the Queen's palace, and it was also said that some of the vegetables for the Fuentes' soups came from the royal gardens. That story, Tabetha had decided to believe, as she liked the idea of tasting royal tomatoes and leeks when she ate her bowl of soup in the humble inn. As for the Witch rumours, they were definitely nonsense, as all Fuentes women had black eyes, and everyone knew that the eyes of Witches were green with catlike pupils. Who cared anyway, as long as she was not the child-eating kind? The soups the Fuenteses served made one believe the world was a benevolent place. That was worth taking the risk that a Witch served them. And, they accepted the coins she found by the river as payment.

The small restaurant was as warm and welcoming as usual on this cold Christmas Eve, and no one found it surprising that the walls were covered with letters and postcards from guests who had found the feeling of home at the plain wooden tables. Most of them came from places Tabetha had never heard of, and they all held the promise the river murmured to her when she was scavenging its muddy shores: that the world was vast and filled with miraculous things, creatures and places.

"Good evening. Could I get some of that spicy bean soup, please?" she asked, chasing a Grass Elf, barely bigger than a coin, from her forehead. Their dust was in high demand, as it gave sweet dreams, but Tabetha couldn't afford to get lost in them. Those dreams were only lies anyway, and waking up from them only made facing reality harder.

Ofelia Fuentes used her left hand to inspect the three slightly bent coins Tabetha had put on the counter. It was her only hand. Ofelia Fuentes's right arm ended shortly under the elbow, but one soon forgot that when watching her move swiftly behind the counter.

"Keep that one," she said, handing one of the coins back to Tabetha. "You may get more than a soup for that, from the collectors on Celt Street." She had quite a deep voice for a girl, and her accent made even plain words sound somehow mysterious. "The other two are fine," she said to the Hob who was filling the bowls.

The portion was even bigger than usual.

"Our Christmas Eve portion," Ofelia commented, pushing the bowl over the counter.

Christmas. None of the men and women at the tables seemed to care. Tabetha remembered how, on their first Christmas in Londra, her mother had taken her to the big tree in front of the Queen's palace. It'd had so many living lights in it: Hobs, Will-o'-the-Wisps and swarms of Grass and Water Elves. Her mother had always wrapped something up for Tabetha—even if it was only an old toy, she would make it look new by adding some ribbon or bird feathers.

The drunken guest had returned to his table, but he was yelling at everyone in a language Tabetha didn't know. Ofelia Fuentes kept her calm, but when he banged his fist down on his plate so violently that it broke, she merely cast a glance at the kitchen door and he left without any further demonstrations of anger.

Tabetha wondered whether the Fuentes themselves had spread the tale about the Troll in their kitchen.

She took her time eating her soup—although her hunger didn't make it an easy task—all the while hoping Ofelia's mother would show up, but she didn't. Outside, the snow was once again falling densely, and one could hear the wind sing a chilly Christmas song in the narrow street overlooking the river. So there was even more protest than usual when the Hobs rang the rusty bell on the wall, which told everyone it was closing time.

"Do you always eat this slowly?" Ofelia Fuentes asked, when the tables were finally empty and Tabetha was still sitting at the counter, scraping the last remains of her soup out of her bowl. "Is the soup not to your liking today?"

"Where's your mother?" Tabetha asked.

Ofelia nodded at the Hobs, and they jumped onto each other's shoulders to lock the door.

31

"She went back to Metagirta, where most of our family lives. She can't stand the cold. She complains about it all day long. Sometimes she's gone for months. One never knows. Why? Are you one of those people who need her advice to get through life? My father says my mother draws them like moths to a flame."

Tabetha cast her a cold glance, and swallowed her question of whether Mister Fuentes really worked for the Queen.

Ofelia walked over to the table where the angry guest had sat, and gathered the broken pieces of his plate with her one hand. Tabetha was almost tempted to offer to help. Almost. But, as Tabetha never asked for help herself, she resisted the temptation.

"What's your name?" Ofelia's eyes were as black as a piece of coal.

"Ted."

"Ted what?"

"Brown."

"Ah, *marrón*. That's what you'd be called in our language." Ofelia put the broken pieces of plate onto the counter. "It sounds better, doesn't it? Our last name means 'fountains'.

Very appropriate for a gardener, my father always says. I guess it even fits a soup kitchen, somehow." She wiped some soup from the counter. "So… what did you want my mother's advice on?"

Tabetha hesitated. She was not sure she liked this girl, and she really didn't know her at all. But who else could she ask?

"There was a man on the river bank today," she began. "He said he'll pay three silver shillings if I find a shard of this glass." She pulled the clipping out of her pocket. "Do you know what's so special about it?"

Ofelia looked at the clipping. "Did he say his name, the man?"

"Bartholomew something."

"Bartholomew Jakes. Oh yes. He always shows up around Christmas." Ofelia filled a bowl with soup and reached for a spoon. "He's a treasure hunter. Sometimes there's a dozen of them down by the river at this time of year. I've no idea why they believe they'll find the glass around here. It isn't exactly the nicest part of the embankment."

A treasure hunter, of course. Tabetha felt quite stupid that she hadn't figured it out

33

herself. Hunting for magical objects — Arthur's Sword, Sleeping Beauty's Bed, Rapunzel's Hair, a Kelpie's Hoof — and selling them to the rich and powerful was a well-rewarded trade, for there was nothing more desirable in this world than the power that true magic could grant. What better job could there be? However, Tabetha was quite sure being a treasure hunter was another job women weren't allowed.

"So, that glass" — she said, making her voice sound as if she didn't care a bit — "it can do real magic? Not the fake kind all those false Witches sell at Seven Dials?" When Ofelia Fuentes gave her a long, enquiring look, Tabetha quickly lowered her head — but she obviously wasn't as good at concealing things as she believed.

"Oh look at you!" Ofelia uttered a soft laugh. "I think you already found a piece!" She leant over the counter, casting the Hobs a quick glance. They were known for their gossiping. "Congratulations," she whispered. "That's quite a find. The glass which Jakes is looking for… it's called the Glass of Lead and Gold. There's always talk about it around this time of year, as it's supposed to work its magic only on Christmas Day."

The Glass of Lead and Gold? It didn't sound too promising. Especially the lead part.

"What does it do?" asked Tabetha. Everyone knew a Witch's Comb turned you into a bird, and a Table of Plenty filled itself with food whenever you needed it. But, a glass?

Ofelia Fuentes shrugged her shoulders. "They say it makes the miserable rich, whatever that means. But there are lots of stories about the glass."

"What stories?"

Ofelia put a few dirty glasses into the sink and signalled for the Hobs to wipe them dry. "Last Christmas, the newspaper that clipping comes from wrote that the Fairies made the glass. The ones who disappeared when all their lakes froze over. But those journalists come up with a new story about it every Christmas."

"You read newspapers?" Tabetha had never heard of a woman who did. Her mother certainly hadn't.

Ofelia shrugged her shoulders. "I got into the habit when my father had me wrap

35

elfenflower bulbs in old newspaper pages. He got quite upset when he caught me reading instead of working, but those moods never last long with him, and now he buys me a newspaper every morning."

She scooped a Hob out of the soup water with her handless arm. It had slipped on the wet counter.

"This Christmas," she said, while throwing a towel over him, "they quoted an antiques dealer who swears an Alderelf made the glass and threw it into the river on purpose, to make the Themse deliver it as a very special Christmas present. It sounds like a silly tale to me, but who knows? People say many terrible things about those Elves—this is a nice story, for a change."

Alderelves, Fairies… People talked about them all the time, but nobody ever saw them, and Tabetha very much hoped that none of them existed. Who wanted immortals around—creatures who were far more powerful than any human could ever be and, if the tales were true, deadly cruel and scheming? Her mother had talked about them all her life, especially about the Mirrors of Magic, which the Alderelves had supposedly built for travel to another world. "That world is almost like ours," she had whispered into Tabetha's ear, cradling her in her arms against the cold, in the miserable basement room where Tabetha had watched her die. "But Londra is called London and the houses are all as shiny as the palace of the Queen, made from glass and silver. There are no Gold Ravens there to curse you, no Mermaids luring poor fishermen like your father to their deaths, no Thumblings, who steal the little you have. Only normal people, who eat and drink whatever they want and never get sick or old."

Tabetha had always thought she would miss the Thumblings and Mermaids, and even the Gold Ravens. Once, her mother had believed she had spotted one of those magical mirrors through the window of an antiques shop. Tabetha still remembered how she had dragged her through the door. The frame of the mirror was covered in silver roses, as the Mirrors of Magic were described, but before her mother could touch the glass, the shop owner had dragged them both back. Nowadays, Tabetha sometimes sold him the coins she found. He didn't recognize her in her boys' clothes, of course. He probably didn't even remember grabbing her mother and pushing her out his door so hard that she hurt her knees on the cobblestones. But Tabetha remembered, and she never brought the really old coins to him.

Ofelia Fuentes washed the last glass and handed it to the Hob, who was still trying to dry his soaked clothes with the towel. Hobs were always impeccably dressed, in suits and dresses that often copied the clothes worn by servants in rich households. Another one emerged from the kitchen, using the Hob-flap in the door. He climbed up Ofelia's dress, jumped onto her shoulders and whispered something into her ear. Ofelia nodded, as she handed the newspaper clipping back to Tabetha. The nails on her one hand were painted red and green. Maybe she liked Christmas? Or maybe she was just making fun of it. It was hard to read those black eyes.

"Tell her to stay," Tabetha heard her say to the Hob. "I may need her later on."

The Hob nodded and disappeared again through the kitchen door, while Ofelia chased a Dust Elf from her nose. When their wings caught the light, they shimmered in all the colours of the rainbow.

"If you want my advice, although it's not my mother's: don't tell anyone you found a piece of that glass."

"Of course not. How foolish do you think I am?"

"Well, you told me."

Oh, Tabetha was really not sure she liked this girl.

"Though just a shard probably won't do anything anyway." Ofelia took another spoon from the bowl she had filled for herself. "I am sure you need to make it into a new glass to make the magic work."

Of course. Tabetha was very irritated with herself for not having thought about that.

"Do you like to dress like that?" Ofelia pointed at Tabetha's coarse pants and jacket.

Tabetha froze. "What are you talking about?" She couldn't help but sound hoarse with embarrassment.

Ofelia looked straight into her eyes, so that Tabetha didn't know how to return her gaze.

"Nobody notices, right? Because people are stupid."

Ofelia raised her handless left arm and wiped a Will-o'-the-Wisp off her cheek. "They look at you, and they don't really see you. But I do. 'Ofelia,' my mother always says, 'don't look too closely at the world.' How? I always wondered how it feels to have short hair. It takes me ages each morning to brush mine."

Tabetha was not sure how she felt. Relieved, that someone knew? Or irritation that her secret had been revealed so bluntly? "It keeps the lice away," she replied coolly. *And the hands of men*, Tabetha added in her head. Although she wasn't sure whether Ofelia Fuentes would appreciate that effect. What was the lipstick for, and the rouge, if not to draw those hands?

"And I like my clothes," she added. "I always found dresses annoying. My father wouldn't take me on his boat, because one drowns in them more easily." Not that his clothes had saved him, nor the strength of men, which he had taken so much pride in.

"Your hair looks as if it would be beautiful if you ever let it grow." Ofelia drove her hand through her chestnut hair. "I always wanted red hair. Like the Witches." She wore her hair up like a grown-up woman. Tabetha had to admit that she liked the look of it, and the glow the Will-o'-the-Wisps gave it. She tried to imagine herself like that, with a tight dress instead of the layers that hid her growing breasts, red lips and...

... one hand.

Ofelia pulled the lace of her sleeve over her left arm. She seemed to not care at all, but maybe she remembered it when she talked to someone she didn't know well?

"If you want, I can take you to a glass-blower—the one who fixes our broken bowls and glasses."

Tabetha pushed the clipping back into one of her pouches. "Thank you," she murmured. "I'll think about it."

But she wouldn't. The services of a glass-blower were far too expensive. *Never mind*, she told herself, to take the sting out of her disappointment. *I can still sell the shard to that treasure hunter for three silver shillings. And the magic is probably not that powerful anyway, considering what it's called.*

41

Two of the Hobs had started a fight on the counter. When they pushed Tabetha's empty bowl over the edge, Ofelia stopped them with a few sharp words. Hobs love to fight. They are much stronger than their size suggests; so strong that some men made them fight dogs for bets. Even the Queen was said to love watching those fights. Limpey claimed she'd had an arena built in her palace especially for it, and that the Hobs survived surprisingly often, although the only weapon they were allowed to carry was a sewing needle.

"Fighting Hobs, and angry guests... Something always gets broken here." Ofelia watched, with a frown, as the Hobs cleaned away the remains of the bowl. "That one is lost, but what if I take the broken things that still have a chance to the glass-blower and pretend your shard is just one of mine, to evade any questions?"

Outside, the snow was still falling. Some of the flakes clung to the windows — Snow men and Snow women, their fragile bodies shimmering like crystals. They could spread a delicious warmth in your hands if you managed to catch one, but you had to be very careful as their limbs were as sharply edged as razors.

Don't trust anybody, Tabetha. Those words were the only heritage Tabetha's mother had left her, along with an old scarf. She had whispered them with her last breath, and Tabetha had tried to follow her advice. But it's hard to live that way, and one day she'd been so lonely that she trusted an older boy. He had sold her to the chimney sweep, who lit a fire beneath her when she didn't climb fast enough. Why would she trust a girl she barely knew, who had a strange accent and painted the fingernails of her one hand red and green?

"Okay," Tabetha murmured. "Where is this glass-blower's place? On Crystal Lane?" Most of them were.

"Yes, number twenty-three. Do you have the shard on you?"

Tabetha shook her head with a contemptuous smile. Of course not. Only fools kept their finds on them.

"You want me to come with you and get it?" Ofelia asked. "Christmas doesn't make the streets of this city any safer, and this shard may prove to be quite a valuable piece."

"No, that's fine," Tabetha said. *Don't trust anyone.* "I'm used to being on my own." *And I doubt a one-handed girl in a nice dress would be much help.*

"Dip the shard in the snow," Ofelia called after her. "If it doesn't melt, it is not what you think. At least, that's what the newspapers say."

AFTER THE WARMTH INSIDE THE INN, the cold cut through Tabetha's rags like a razor, a sharp reminder that it was not good to get spoilt by staying inside so long. Even the moon was hanging above the roofs like a piece of ice, and Tabetha was grateful the place where she hid her finds was not too far away. Like most mudlarks, she kept her treasures a safe distance from where she slept, as thieves could follow her there too easily. The streets were crowded with families and carol-singers, and beggars who hoped for mercy on Christmas Eve. Toymakers were selling their tin soldiers and music boxes from brightly coloured carts, and starving musicians played the songs of the season, more or less well, with their frozen fingers. At first, Tabetha stopped at every corner—as was her routine, to make sure no one followed her—but she soon gave up on that, as it was impossible to spot anyone in the river of faces floating through the city.

Not everything mudlarks dig out from the mud sells, but they all kept some of those finds nevertheless. Sometimes, the fragment of a glazed plate granted a glimpse at a time long-forgotten or at the world beyond their grasp, where people ate with silver spoons from beautifully painted crockery. Tabetha kept her treasures safe in an empty barrel in the overgrown backyard of an abandoned house whose brick walls were marked by a fire. The bakery sign still swung on rusty chains beside a boarded-up door at the front, and the old woman who often sat on the stairs in front of the house next door told everyone the house had burnt down because the baker had been so drunk that he'd fallen asleep next to his oven.

The snow was piled high between the blackened walls of the yard and when Tabetha had finally dug the barrel out of the snow, she was even more relieved than usual that the wooden box she kept inside was untouched. It was also a gift of the river. All mudlarks believed the Themse to be a living thing who, following unpredictable moods, either gave or took away, and they all regularly threw something precious back into the murky waters, to pay the river back and make sure it meant them well.

Tabetha's wooden box held a myriad of treasures, including a broken clay pipe with a faun's face—which she loved so much that she had never managed to sell it—a small fragment of delicate white china with a blue pattern that to her eyes resembled a dragon's tail, and a coin with strange letters, which she had told herself had come from an ancient tribe of warriors who were all ginger-haired like herself. The broken silver chain with the small moonstones was a rare find. Most of the city's lost jewellery was snatched up by the Toshers, scavengers who searched the sewers. Luckily, some valuables ended up in the river nevertheless, as had the ring that lay next to the chain and sadly didn't fit any of Tabetha's fingers. Amongst these favoured items was the piece of glass she had come for, so delicate that she'd always wondered how it had survived the river.

Usually, the glass fragments she found in the mud were thick, and often pale greenish or brown, but this one was like a thin slice of frozen air. The delicately engraved lines portraying Fairies and Elves felt like fine threads of silver, when you ran your finger over them. Tabetha barely dared to take the shard out of the box, knowing how precious it might be. It felt very cold between her fingers, but when she dipped it into the snow, as Ofelia had suggested, the glass melted it as efficiently as a piece of hot coal.

How her heart began to race! One often heard stories about objects with magical powers: the Witches' Combs, the sticks that beat up your enemies, or the tables that served you food at any time. The Queen was supposed to have a vast collection. But Tabetha had never met anyone who actually possessed such a magical thing. She put the shard back into the box and closed the wooden lid. The box was slightly warped from its time in the water, and the river had left its marks on the dark wood.

She leant against the barrel and stared up at the pale coin of the moon. *Don't trust anyone, Tabetha.* Could she trust Ofelia Fuentes? Surprisingly, her heart's answer was a firm yes. *Well, that heart of yours also trusted the boy who sold you to the chimney sweep*, she told herself. *So what does that tell you about your heart?*

"Look at that!"

The voice Tabetha heard behind her sounded familiar.

"The young mud rat inspects his treasures. May I have a look? I am quite sure I may be very interested in one of them."

Tabetha turned around.

Bartholomew Jakes gave her a nasty smile. "You're quite a good liar, until you get excited about something someone shows you." He pointed at the Thumbling who was peeking out of his coat pocket. "I had him follow you. He is a treacherous little thief, but an excellent spy when fed well, and so good at being invisible. He was barely a step away from you when you talked to that one-handed girl. Give it to me. The glass. Come on, it's cold."

A snowflake landed on the black leather of his glove, as he stretched out his hand.

Tabetha closed her frozen fingers even more firmly around the box in her lap. No. The river had given the glass to her.

"Don't tell me I have to slit your throat on Christmas, boy!" The treasure hunter pushed his coat back to reveal a belt and a knife handle. "You know what? I'll give you two pence if you give it to me without making this complicated. After all, it's Christmas Eve."

"The river gave it to me. It won't work for you anyway."

"The river?" Bartholomew Jakes uttered a joyless laugh. "Did you hear that, Thumbs? Believe me, I have a lot of experience with

49

treasure that didn't come to me willingly. It always works. Magic doesn't care who you are or whether you deserve it."

The Thumbling giggled, and scrutinized Tabetha with his pale yellow eyes. A Thumbling had stolen the first penny she had earned as a mudlark.

"Come on." Bartholomew Jakes took a step forward. "It's as cold as a vampire's tomb tonight. Hand me that miserable box of yours! I am sure nothing in it is worth dying for."

Merry Christmas, Tabetha. The world was a terrible place.

Two men were coming down the road, Tabetha saw them pass the remains of the wall that had once surrounded the baker's backyard. But who would they believe if she called for help? The man with the expensive boots, of course. There would be many people in the houses to her left and right, but people in these quarters of the city were too busy struggling to stay alive themselves to help anyone else.

A woman had stopped right by the gap in the burnt-down wall that still held the rusty hinge of a gate long gone. She was huge. Even from this distance, she looked almost as tall as the Giantlings guarding the Queen's palace. *What are you looking at?* Tabetha wanted to call over to her. *Are you waiting for them to kill me? That would be quite a festive entertainment on Christmas Eve, wouldn't it?*

The woman stepped through the gap and came walking towards them, with slow and heavy steps which made Tabetha think of her as a tree that had grown legs. The deep snow made even those heavy steps as silent as a cat's, but Thumblings are known for their sharp ears and the one in Bartholomew Jakes's pocket alerted his master with a shrill squeal. The treasure hunter turned around, reaching for his pistol.

The woman stopped, just a few steps away from him.

Her skin gave her away. She was a Troll. One didn't meet them often in the streets, as they liked to keep to themselves, but Tabetha had once seen one at the harbour, carrying huge wooden crates onto a ship as if he carried sacks of feathers. His skin had resembled the wood of the ship's hull. The Troll woman's skin was darker and rough like oak bark, while her shoulder-length hair was as pale green as the leaves of a beech in spring.

Everyone knew a Troll could break a man's neck with one finger, even rip off his head without much effort. Tabetha wasn't sure whether that was also true for their women, but Bartholomew Jakes clearly believed it. The treasure hunter tried to hide his fear — as it was caused by a woman, it was even more embarrassing—but he took a couple of steps back, while pointing his pistol at the Troll. The Thumbling disappeared into the depths of his master's pocket.

"Leaf the boy ulone," the Troll woman said. She said it very calmly, her voice sounding to Tabetha as if it were echoing up out of a well, but she had closed the fingers of her right hand into a fist; a fist as big as Bartholomew Jakes's head.

"I am just doing business with him," he said, still pointing his pistol at the Troll. "He stole that box from me. He can go, once I have it back."

"Don't lie to me, littel man," the Troll woman said. "And put zat pistol away. It makes me vant to punch you, just a littel bit, and it's Christmas."

Tabetha hesitated when the huge woman waved her to her side, but for now even a Troll seemed the safer option. Bartholomew Jakes followed her with his eyes, but he didn't grab her when she walked past him, her box firmly under her arm. From close by, the Troll woman looked even more imposing,

but it felt strangely comforting to stand by her side. Like standing under a big tree.

"Do not follow us," she said to the treasure hunter, "or try to find him. I don't vant to see yur ugly face anyvere near the boy. If I do, I will peel it off yur scull, like potato skin. Understant?"

The treasure hunter spat into the snow. "I hope you cook and eat him," he snapped. "Isn't that what your kind likes to do? Though there may not be enough meat on him for a woman your size."

The Troll woman smiled. Her teeth were almost as green as her hair. "I'm sure you know ull ubout man-eaters. I heer treasur huntars like to plonder zeir caves for the objects ze victims left behind. My aont used to say zat your kind tricks rich travallars into going past un Ogre cave, so he dos ze killing and you only have to wash the blood off zeir belongings."

Bartholomew Jakes pushed his pistol back into his belt.

"There will be another time," he said. "And another place. Life is full of opportunities."

"If yu say so." The Troll woman's hand came down on Tabetha's shoulder, like a huge warm blanket. "Tell zat creature in yur pocket if he sneaks vun more time in ze Fuentes' establishment, I grind his bones and use zem for my chicken soop."

Then she waved for Tabetha to follow her back to the road.

The Troll woman introduced herself as Borga. That was all she said while they made their way to Crystal Lane. Tabetha was grateful for the silence, as she was still quite shaken by the fact she hadn't been able to deal with the treasure hunter alone. She was proud that she had managed to survive without her mother for almost six years, and she hated to be reminded how young and vulnerable she was.

It was a long way to Crystal Lane. They had to leave the poor quarters by the river behind and enter the city of the rich, with its parks and horse carriages, wide roads framed by huge mansions, and policemen on every corner, who usually registered mudlarks with a disgusted sniff. Tabetha rarely entered this part of Londra. Most of the collectors she sold coins or fragments of pottery to lived and worked closer to the river, and she usually felt dirty and poor amongst all the velvet dresses, fur coats and polished boots of the wealthy—but she had never walked through the streets of the rich behind a Troll. It was like following a four-mast ship down the Themse. Most faces became hostile at the sight of the huge woman, but instead of being pushed aside or yelled at, as Tabetha usually experienced in these districts, the fur coats and carriages stopped or hastily made room for them to pass.

When the pair finally reached Crystal Lane, where the glass-blowers had run their workshops for more than seven centuries, Ofelia was already waiting in front of the biggest shop. The number twenty-three was etched in gold into the panels of its ornate front door.

Borga gave Ofelia a nod, and murmured: "I need to get back to my soops." Then she disappeared into the next side street, ploughing her way past a Dwarf woman who sold hot chestnuts at the corner and a man who nearly dropped a water barrel when he saw her.

"I hope Borga didn't rip off any limbs or break any skulls?" Ofelia asked. "She's a good cook, but she has a bit of a temper."

"I didn't need her help," Tabetha said. Her pride was hurt and she still cursed herself for not having looked over her shoulder more often or spotting that treacherous Thumbling at the Soup Kitchen. Her only comfort was that Ofelia hadn't either.

"Of course. None of us need help, right?" Ofelia replied, reaching into the basket she was carrying. She brought forth a pair of boots. "A guest threw them at me, so I kept them. They're far from pretty, but as you don't care about that anyway… I stuffed the toes with paper, as I'm sure they're too big for you."

No thanks, Tabetha wanted to say. *If I need better shoes, I'll buy myself some. Who are you, to give me boots and send your Troll woman after me? I was fine all these years without you.* But her feet were so cold by now inside her wet, worn-out shoes that she was worried she might lose a toe, like Limpey, and the boots looked rather new and not bad at all.

"I'll find some coins to pay for them," she said, as she took her leaking boots off and slipped into the boots Ofelia had brought. "Has that Troll woman always lived with your family?" It felt good to have dry feet.

58

"No. My father helped her with something. They don't talk about it, but since then Borga's cooked for us. Did you bring the shard?"

Tabetha closed her arms firmly around the wooden box. "Yes."

"Here." Ofelia handed her a napkin. "Wrap it in there and put it in my basket. As I said, I think it's better we pretend it's mine."

"Why?" *Don't trust anybody, Tabetha.*

Ofelia looked up to the dark sky. It had begun to snow again. "I have only one hand," she said, without looking at Tabetha. "Try tying shoelaces with one hand. Or putting up your hair. I have to ask for help from time to time. Maybe that makes it easier for me to trust people."

Maybe. And maybe trusting people was easier when your father worked for the Queen, Tabetha thought, but she opened the wooden box and wrapped the small piece of glass into the napkin.

"Let me do the talking," Ofelia said, while Tabetha placed the shard in her basket. "Arthur Soames is not a nice man, and around Christmas he's in an especially foul mood.

He claims it is because so many of the tree ornaments he makes get broken, but I think he doesn't need a reason. He's just as bitter as juniper juice."

A dozen colourful glass bells chimed above the shop door, when Ofelia opened it. The man inside reminded Tabetha of an angry gingerbread man, with his balding head, round-cheeked face, raisin eyes and lips pressed so tightly against each other that they could have been a line of sugar icing. He was arranging a few tall vases on a shelf.

"Ofelia Fuentes! Not you again!" he snapped. "Tell your mother to teach you that you shouldn't allow your guests to break your glasses on each other's foolish heads!"

He gave Tabetha's worn clothes such a disapproving look that she was tempted to break one of the vases he had arranged on his gingerbread head, but she had to admit his shop was filled with miraculous objects more beautiful than any glass she had ever seen. The Christmas tree, which claimed almost a third of the shop, was covered in glass baubles in every colour of the rainbow. Glass angels, with delicate wings, hung from its evergreen branches, alongside miniature glass parcels with glass ribbons and bows, glass Unicorns, glass Mermaids and

61

even glass Dragons. When Tabetha couldn't resist touching one of the Fairies, Arthur Soames grabbed her arm and roughly pulled her back.

"I don't allow street ruffians into my shop, Ofelia," he said. "Who is this? Another charity project of your mother's?"

Oh yes, Tabetha wanted to break more than one vase on his head.

"He's as hard-working as you, Arthur," Ofelia replied, emptying her basket onto Arthur Soames's counter.

"Is that why he smells of dead fish and ship oil?" The glass-blower straightened one of the Dragons on the Christmas tree, and stepped behind his counter. "How many glasses is it, this time?"

"Ten. And six bowls. And... this." The shard caught the gas light that lit the store like a piece of ice, when Ofelia unwrapped it.

Arthur Soames bent over it and didn't say anything for a long time.

"Good heavens," he finally murmured. "That's a piece of—"

"No, sadly it's not," Ofelia interrupted him. "It's only a piece of a copy. They were quite in fashion when my mother was young, as you may recall. But the glass holds great sentimental value for her, as it was a present from her father, and now one of the Hobs has broken it. Please, Mr Soames. I need it fixed before she comes back from Metagirta."

Oh what a brilliant liar she was. Even Tabetha almost believed her.

Arthur Soames took a magnifying glass out of a drawer. Its gold-framed lens was bigger than Tabetha's fist. "I never understood how a woman as reasonable as your mother can bear to work with Hobs," he murmured, while inspecting the shard through the thick lens. "They are pea-brained and utterly childish. A copy, you say... Well, it is astonishingly well done. The engravings are undoubtedly a master's work."

"Yes, my mother was always very proud of it." Ofelia's voice was calm, as if she was not at all troubled by Arthur Soames's inquisitiveness. Tabetha couldn't help but admire this.

"Your mother is a flower, who withers in our endless rains. But I guess your father is used to keeping tropical plants alive in our climate. I heard the Queen likes them very much." When the glass-blower turned the shard to inspect it from another angle, Tabetha saw that his fingers were covered with blisters, which she supposed shouldn't be surprising, considering his fiery work.

"I once made your mother a sun decoration for her Christmas tree," Arthur Soames murmured. "It had ninety-nine beams blown from pale-yellow glass. I wonder what became of it. I am sure those foolish Hobs broke it as well." He lifted his head. "Where are the other pieces of this copy?"

"That sun still hangs on our tree," Ofelia replied. "But the Hobs threw all the other pieces away, to cover up their accident. I was lucky I found this one under my mother's bed."

The lies left her lips so easily, as if she plucked them out of thin air!

"It is one advantage of our winters that the Hob population is always decimated," Arthur Soames stated. "I am sure the last typhoid epidemic was caused by Hobs. They don't wash, and they multiply like mice. It makes me shudder to even imagine one of them in my workshop."

"Then who helps you with the fire and the oven?" Tabetha's curiosity had overruled her dislike of this man. "Is your glass made only by humans?"

Arthur Soames looked as surprised as if a fish had begun to talk. "Every decent glassblower works exclusively with Fire Elves. They make the glass melt much faster and are able to handle it without burning their hands."

He placed the shard into a small box and placed that next to Ofelia's broken bowls and glasses.

"Making a new glass with an existing shard is a very difficult process, and I will have to match the pattern, so…" He frowned and scribbled some numbers on a sheet of paper. "One shilling for the glass, three pence to fix the rest. And in case you intend to ask: no, I don't grant discounts at Christmas."

Tabetha saw Ofelia draw in a deep breath. One shilling. You would have to sell many bowls of soup to earn that. But, once again, Ofelia's voice sounded unimpressed when she replied: "That's fine. Can I pay half now and half next week?"

Arthur Soames frowned, and cast a glance at the shard. "As long as you don't tell anybody I've been lenient," he snapped. "Everything will be done by tomorrow. One of my shop boys will drop the delivery off, although I am sure they'll moan I have them work on Christmas Day."

He pointed at Ofelia's handless arm, when she slipped the handle of her empty basket over it. "I told your mother I can make you a beautiful hand from glass. I made her a good price."

Ofelia gave him a smile as cold as the snowflakes whirling past his shop windows. "Thank you, Mr Soames. But I would break off a finger within a week," she said. "And after all, there are far fewer one-handed girls in this town than two-handed ones. Merry Christmas."

A GROUP OF CAROL-SINGERS WERE singing in front of the shop next door, when Ofelia closed Arthur Soames's door behind them. The singers' clothes were covered with flickering swarms of Will-o'-the-Wisps. A bit of honey did the trick. Tabetha knew that from No-teeth Harry, who spent the evenings as a carol-singer and claimed it earned him twice of what he made with mudlarking. But he was blessed with an angel's voice, though there was otherwise nothing angelic about him.

How did you lose your hand? The question had lingered on Tabetha's tongue since she first laid eyes on Ofelia. She had managed to swallow it down several times, but it just wanted to get out, like something that burnt her mouth. Ofelia seemed to sense this. She gave her a look that said "not you as well" and made her wish she had tried harder to hide her interest.

"I was born like this," Ofelia said. "Maybe you were born dressing like a boy?" She wrapped her scarf around her neck so swiftly that for a moment Tabetha could have sworn she had two hands. "You want to wait at the inn, or do you have a warmer place you call home?"

The Will-o'-the-Wisps blurred in front of Tabetha's eyes. Tears. *Look at you!* she scolded herself. *Just a bit of Christmas spirit and you're losing it.*

"It's actually not that warm a place," she said hoarsely. "And I wouldn't call it home."

"Well, then I suggest you come with me," Ofelia said.

But when she turned, Tabetha was still standing in front of Arthur Soames's shop door. "I'll pay you back," she told the older girl. "Every penny. It will take a while, but I will."

"Not if we both freeze to death tonight," Ofelia answered. "Hurry up, or I'll regret I asked you to come along."

But Tabetha still didn't move. "You're a very good liar."

Ofelia looked at her, with night-black eyes.

"I am," she said. "I love to make up lies. It's like making up stories. My father says I should be a writer one day. A left-handed one, of course."

She turned again, and started walking.

Tabetha still hesitated, but eventually she followed her. After all, it was a very cold night.

Tabetha slept on a bench in the Fuentes' kitchen. It was by far the warmest place she had slept for years. Borga was still cooking when they arrived back at the inn. Her head almost hit the ceiling, as the house was one of the oldest in Londra, having survived the last fire. The ten Hobs who helped her—men, women and children—all had to fit on one of the wooden chopping boards. Some were complaining, in their bird-like voices, that they would have to work until dawn to complete all the Christmas orders the Fuentes had accepted, but the Troll woman shut them up with one impatient grunt, and Tabetha fell asleep to the sound of her humming a tune that sounded both sad and astonishingly harmonic.

THE TROLL WOMAN WAS GONE WHEN Tabetha woke, and the Hobs were sleeping amongst stacks of clean pots and pans. Morning light was seeping through the window and a few Grass Elves were dancing in the pale sun, but they hadn't brought Tabetha sweet dreams. She couldn't remember much of what her dream had been about, but it had definitely been a bad one, featuring Arthur Soames and Bartholomew Jakes's

Thumbling. Ofelia had been in it too—with six hands, each holding a glass.

She was nowhere to be seen, when Tabetha looked for her in the restaurant. A girl named Sue, who she had seen behind the counter a few times before, told her Ofelia had gone out. Nothing more. She wasn't back when the girl opened the door for the first guests, and neither did Arthur Soames's delivery boy show up. After waiting more than two hours, Tabetha was tempted to go down to the river—as its steadily moving waters always calmed her mind—but she was afraid her delivery would arrive in her absence, so she stayed and waited.

And waited.

And waited.

And waited.

It was already early afternoon when Ofelia came back, her cheeks as red as her lips from the cold. *Where have you been?* Tabetha wanted to ask, but she didn't. *It will be fine*, she told herself. She even managed to smile at Ofelia, but Ofelia didn't smile back. She barely said a word to Tabetha, almost as if they'd never met, and for the next two hours Tabetha didn't catch more than a few vacant glances from her, while she watched Ofelia serve soup to sailors and dockworkers, with a smile on her face that didn't reach her eyes.

You don't know her at all, Tabetha's heart whispered. Or whatever it was that whispered inside her sometimes. *How could you trust her, after having just met her? How? Why?* She asked herself these questions over and over again, as she felt more and more invisible in the crowded restaurant and Ofelia's eyes evaded her like those of the rich women who passed her on the street. She should have known. The dress, the lipstick, even the accent… and all those brilliant lies! And Tabetha had trusted her with the one valuable object she owned.

At three of chimes, the small restaurant was so crowded that there was a line at the door, but there was still no delivery.

There wasn't one at four, or at five, when the lantern man lit the gas lights outside. Ofelia was serving a man whose face was covered in tattoos of Mermaids and Watermen, when Tabetha grabbed her arm.

"Why is the glass not here?"

The tattooed man gave her a sinister look. The customers would all take Ofelia's side, she realized, not the mudlark who had escaped from the cold and slept on the kitchen bench.

"I don't know. Maybe it didn't work. Maybe the shard was not enough." Ofelia didn't look at her. She sounded tired and as if she was somewhere else.

Or like someone who had a secret.

"You made a deal with Mr Soames! That's why his boy didn't show up. That's why you had your Troll follow me! You planned it from the beginning."

"Planned what?" Ofelia freed her arm, with a strength that surprised Tabetha.

"You stole it from me! That's what you did. 'Let's pretend the shard is mine.' I bet you

72

told Soames to deliver the glass only once the stupid mudlark is gone!"

The man with the tattoos placed himself behind Ofelia. The Mermaids on his forehead moved. Rubbing Elven dust into the skin had that effect.

"That's a wild tale." Ofelia's voice was like ice. "I didn't know you were such a great storyteller."

"I'm definitely not as great a storyteller as you—or should I say, liar!" Tabetha hated the words she said, but she hated feeling like a fool even more. "That glass was meant to be mine. It's the first time something good came to me, and you stole it!"

Ofelia just looked at her with those black eyes, so different from the goose-grey eyes Tabetha's mother had passed on to her.

"Ungrateful! Zat's wat you are!"

All the guests drew their heads down between their shoulders, including the tattooed man. Borga was standing in the open kitchen door. She filled the doorframe more tightly than the door itself.

"But of coars. Yu are just uh mean, silly mud boy, 'oo smells of fish. Leaf her alon!"

She came out from behind the counter, her fists swinging in the air. Tabetha imagined she could feel them all over her already, but Borga stopped when Ofelia stepped in her way.

"She's not even a boy!" she said. "So who's the liar? She trusts nobody. And she only cares about herself. Let her go. I don't care what she says."

She gave Tabetha one more glance with those black eyes, then she turned and chased the Hobs—who had been stood still on the counter as if winter had frozen them—back to work.

"I should have known! A one-handed girl..." Tabetha hated her own voice—so shrill and hurt, like a child's. She even felt like a child again, like the girl sitting by her dead mother's side, all alone, for ever. So angry, so scared. Curse Christmas. It made it all come back. But she couldn't stop. "Yes, a one-handed girl!" she yelled. "I'm sure it was a lie you were born like that! Chopping off a hand, that's the punishment for thieves!"

Borga took a heavy step forward.

"Get out!" she bellowed.

Some of the guests shuffled their feet, not sure if the order was meant for them too.

"You have no hands at all, Tabetha Brown," Ofelia said calmly. "And you don't even know it."

Her words followed Tabetha outside. Ofelia slammed the door so fiercely behind her that the metal sign swung against the façade of the old house, making a sound as hollow as a funeral bell.

THIS TIME, WHEN SHE MADE HER WAY back to Crystal Lane, Tabetha didn't follow a Troll woman who ploughed a path through the crowds, but Christmas had finally emptied the streets and filled the houses. After half an hour of running through the deserted city, she stood once again in front of Arthur Soames's shop, out of breath and with shaking knees, her lungs filled with so much of the icy air that she couldn't stop coughing.

The shop was dark, except for the Will-o'-the-Wisps in the tree, and there was a *CLOSED* sign hanging behind the glass of the door.

Tabetha felt her stomach turn with despair. For once, the river had tried to make up for all the past years of misery, and she had thrown its gift away, giving in to her accursed yearning for trust and love.

She had bent down to pick up a stone to smash Arthur Soames's precious windows with, when she remembered a skill Midget had taught her, just a few weeks before the Waterman killed him. It took her a while to find a hairpin between the cobblestones, but she did, and after a few attempts, the lock at Arthur Soames's shop door gave in.

The glass ornaments on the Christmas tree shimmered even more mysteriously in the dark, but Tabetha felt like breaking them all. She found a door behind the counter, and behind the door a steep staircase leading down to another, metal door in the basement. There was light seeping out under it, and she could feel heat coming through the metal, as if the entrance of Hell was hidden in Arthur Soames's cellar.

The door wasn't locked. Tabetha opened it just wide enough to peek through. What she saw made her almost close the door again. The windowless room behind it was swarming with Fire Elves, like a beehive with bees. Fire-Elf stings were supposed to be deadly, and their fierce, red faces gave the impression that they couldn't wait to use them. Tabetha only dared to slip through the door when they all gathered around a stone basin at the back of the room, which was filled with melted glass.

The Fire Elves hummed with excitement, while some of them pulled strings of the hot mass up like liquid yarn and carried them to a shelf with half-finished bowls and vases. Tabetha couldn't take her eyes off them. She only noticed Arthur Soames when one of the Elves accidentally let a small splash of the melted glass drop on his shoulder. He didn't notice. Arthur Soames was sitting at a workbench, a glass with a slender stem in front of him. He was staring at it, as motionless as if he had done so for hours. Only when Tabetha approached the table, did he lift his head.

"Ah. It's you," he said. "I guess there is no question how you got in. You looked to me like a thief, the moment you stepped into my shop."

"You're the thief," Tabetha said. "That glass is mine. I found the shard, by the river."

"Did you? Who cares? Do you think anyone will believe you or that one-handed daughter of a woman they call a Witch behind her back? You both lied to me. This is the true Glass of Lead and Gold. I suspected it all along, but the Fire Elves confirmed it. They are drawn to magical objects, and got very excited about that piece of a so-called copy."

Tabetha wasn't really listening. *Or that one-handed daughter of a woman they call a Witch behind her back?* She felt so happy. So ridiculously happy. Until she remembered her own words. All those words she had spat at Ofelia, poison brewed by years of loneliness.

Two Fire Elves were hovering above the finished glass, their huge insect eyes taking up almost half of their faces. The Fire Elves' red bodies reflected on the glass like dancing flames. Arthur Soames's mastery had turned the shard Tabetha had dug out of the river mud into a glass of such perfection that not even she could detect the original piece. The

engravings wove around
it seamlessly, and along the
rim there was a fine line of
gold.

"Yes, look at it! You still
think this is yours?" Arthur
Soames's face glowed with sweat
and pride. "Look what my hands
turned that miserable shard into. The Elves
and I gave it back its shape and beauty, the
true form appropriate to its magic. With you,
it would only have stayed a useless fragment
of its former glory, for ever broken."

"It's still mine," Tabetha repeated, although
the buzzing of the Elves rose like an angry
choir around her. "The river gave it to me,
not you."

The glass-blower picked up the glass and
scrutinized it from all sides. "Ah yes, the
river. And I am sure you believe in those tales
about the immortal Elf, who made this glass
and threw it in there to share his magic with
human trash like you?"

He snapped his fingers and the Fire Elves
surrounded Tabetha so densely that she
could feel their heat on her skin. She tried to

79

remember the cold outside, to help relieve the pain, but she couldn't. All she felt was fire.

"They will kill you if I tell them to," Arthur Soames said. "So behave. You may watch me demonstrating the magic that the Glass of Lead and Gold can do when brought back to life by a master's hand."

He reached for a mug filled with water, and poured some into the glass. Then he drank it all and wiped his paper-thin lips with a handkerchief.

"Now, Arthur!" he said to himself. "It's time to think of something tragic. True heartbreak. Deep misery. How about the death of your father? No… your second wife's passing?"

He touched his cheeks. "Nothing? Well…" He frowned. And smiled. "Oh yes. Much better."

A wet shimmer filled his raisin eyes. "It was the most delicate piece I ever made, and that foolish woman broke it within days."

Tears ran down his cheeks and dropped onto the table.

Arthur Soames stared at the wooden surface as if he expected to see flowers grow from it—and uttered an astonishingly vulgar curse when small pieces of lead appeared where his tears had dripped onto the table. He hastily wiped his eyes with the handkerchief and stared at the grey smear on the fabric. He stared at it for quite a while, the Fire Elves swarming round him.

They had all forgotten about Tabetha, and she had just managed to take two silent steps back to the door, when Arthur Soames lifted his head.

"Come here!" he said, waving her to his side. "Unless you want me to set the Elves back on you?"

Tabetha walked over to the table and stared down at the leaden tears that covered it like tiny pebbles from the river.

"As you saw, the magic works for me as well," he continued. "But not in exactly the way I hoped for. I admit crying is not my reaction to what life throws at me, one of the most accomplished citizens of this great city, but you look miserable enough to produce plenty of tears. I am sure any moment of your existence would give reason to shed them. So why don't we collaborate? You drink from the glass and cry some tears, and we'll share the result?"

Tabetha watched how he filled the glass once again with water. She didn't ask what would happen if she denied Arthur Soames her services. The Fire Elves had clearly enjoyed their task of intimidating her earlier.

The water tasted of fire. And of silver, if there was such a taste. Each time Tabetha wanted to put the glass down the Elves gave off an angry hum until she drank it all.

But you look miserable enough to produce plenty of tears. Her mother's last days had been filled with so much pain, fear and despair that she had cried an ocean of tears. But it was not the death of her mother or father that came to Tabetha's mind in Arthur Soames's workshop, nor the pain in the narrow chimneys, or all those nights filled with hunger and loneliness. The words she had said to Ofelia—those were all she could think about. It was so fresh a pain. She had betrayed the trust of someone who might have become a friend.

The first tears she cried were tears of self pity. Tabetha was embarrassed to realize it, but they were tears of shame as well, of helpless loneliness and all the bitterness which life had brought and poisoned her heart with. Her tears were a river running down her cheeks and dripping from her face, onto Arthur Soames's table. They blurred her eyes so much, at first she didn't even see all the gold.

It filled the table and spilt onto the floor — so much gold, all of it tear-shaped. Sadness, turned into the most precious metal on earth. Some of the Fire Elves found their hot hands covered in melted gold, when they tried to pick the tears up, and Arthur Soames clapped his hands like a boy who'd received just the right gift on Christmas Day.

"Well, look at this!" he exclaimed. "I guess you proved to be useful for the first time in your miserable existence, boy."

"I'm not a boy," Tabetha said, while she was waiting for her heart to feel at least some kind of joy. But it wouldn't. It felt as if it had turned to gold as well.

Arthur Soames carefully picked up three tears, grabbed her hand and let them fall into her palm.

"Here, I think that's more than generous. You can buy a pile of rags from those, and soup till the end of your miserable days. And now go. Before the Elves kill you. They like to do things like that, sadly—at least, the ones I know—and I won't be able to hold them back for much longer."

He mocked her with a thin-lipped smile. Tabetha had never before felt such a yearning to hurt someone. She put the three tears into her pocket and looked at the glass, which was standing on the table, surrounded by her tears.

Her Christmas gift, granted by the Themse...

And suddenly she felt it inside, as if the river had come to protect her. She felt its wide, wet vastness, its waters cooled by the melted snow and by cold oceans far away. Tabetha filled each inch of her body with its murky waters until they cooled the heat of the Elves. Then she grabbed the glass and threw it onto the floor, with all the strength she had, and stamped on its shards with the boots Ofelia Fuentes had brought her, until she had crushed them into nothing but powdered glass.

Even the Fire Elves were surprised. This granted Tabetha a few precious seconds to make it through the door. She heard them coming when she was halfway up the stairs, deafening her ears with their angry buzz. But the river still protected her. She heard its wet roar inside her, cooling her burning skin and keeping the Elves at bay. She broke more glass while running through Arthur Soames's shop. She broke as much as she could, although finally its beauty stopped her. Some of the Elves swarmed after her into the night, but the cold killed them on the spot and they fell into the snow, turning as grey as burnt-out coal.

Tabetha ran down many streets before she dared to stop and lean her back against a wall. Her hands were covered with burns, as were her ragged clothes, and she was sure her face didn't look any better.

She cooled the burns with some snow, before she walked into the Fuentes' Soup Kitchen. The girl called Sue took a shocked step back when she saw her, and some of the guests looked as alarmed as if another Troll had walked in. Ofelia Fuentes stood behind the counter, her lips painted as purple as a violet and with almost as many Will-o'-the-Wisps in her hair as sat in the Queen's tree.

Tabetha was limping, as she made her way past the tables. Her boots were too big and their soles were spiked with glass, so she had run all the way back barefoot. She put the boots on the counter when she reached it, and the three golden tears.

Ofelia touched them with her finger. She was wearing golden nail polish now, for Christmas night.

"So it worked."

"Yes."

"And Soames tried to steal the glass?"

"Yes."

Borga came out of the kitchen. Tabetha was sure that one of the Hobs had alerted the cook to her presence.

"Who tried to cook him?" she asked, pointing at Tabetha's burnt skin.

"Her," Ofelia said. "She's a girl. I told you."

Borga went into the kitchen and came back with five eggs in her huge hand. She cracked them in a bowl and placed it in front of Tabetha.

"Egg, *vite*," she said. "Good for burns."

It was true. Tabetha's skin hurt much less when she smeared the pale pulp on her hands and face. All the customers were watching her, but who cared? She had escaped a swarm of Fire Elves, thanks to the river.

"Looking at those burns, I guess Soames still has the glass?"

Tabetha wiped the egg onto her neck. "Yes. And no."

Two women paid for their soup. One had red hair like Tabetha's. Hers had been that long once too. She missed running her fingers through it.

"I crushed the glass," she said. It hurt to think of it. It had been so beautiful.

Ofelia handed a bowl of soup to an old man, who wore the tattoos of the dock workers on the back of his hands. "Soames will make another one from the splinters."

"Yes. But I don't think he'll be able to restore the pattern." Tabetha took her boots and turned them over. The soles were covered with broken glass. She plucked a few splinters out of the leather and lay them on the counter. Each was barely as big as a fingernail. "Maybe we can take these to another glass-blower."

Ofelia brought out an empty bowl for the splinters, and together they both silently picked the glass out of the worn sole. The remains of the Glass of Lead and Gold.

"And don't forget those." Tabetha picked up two of the golden tears. "They are for you. I need only one."

Ofelia shook her head. "No. Keep them. I don't want them."

"I still have to pay you back for Soames's services."

Ofelia bent her head over the boot sole and plucked out another splinter. "No! My mother won't come home—she's tired of the rain and the cold. I went to tell my father, this morning, but you thought I went to Soames, to steal from you. I don't need your gold."

Tabetha's heart felt so cold. It's hard to lose a friend. Especially when you have only one. She turned around. The customers had forgotten about her. No one remembered her. Nobody missed her. Only the river. There was no other place to go to, despite the gold in her pocket. It wouldn't take away the loneliness.

"She could pay for a room, wis one tear." Borga took the bowl with the glass splinters, and ploughed through them with her fingers. "Yu need help, now yur mozzer is gone."

"She doesn't sleep in rooms," Ofelia said. "She likes the river and the mud more than people, and you heard how she thinks I lost my hand. She's so used to pretending she's someone else that she thinks everyone else does the same…"

Borga pressed her huge fingers against the girl's violet lips.

"No more words," she said. "She came back. Let's cook some soup."

Then she took the bowl of broken glass and waved Ofelia to follow her into the kitchen.

Tabetha took the three golden tears from the counter and put them in her pocket. Then she slipped back into the boots and walked to the door. They still had some glass in them and the raw egg was like a second skin on her burnt face. *She doesn't sleep in rooms...*

She put her hand on the door handle, and looked around at all the people talking and eating and laughing. Or just looking sad. There was a river at the Fuentes' inn, too, she realized. A human river of faces and voices, of joy and sadness, brought forth by this city. At times it could feel cold and threatening, and one could drown in it, as her mother had. But in this very moment, on this Christmas evening, it felt warm and wide and welcoming.

When Tabetha stepped into the kitchen, Borga was pouring a few glass splinters into one of the small muslin wraps that she used to hang spices into her soups. The Hobs were watching her with worried faces.

"Don't look like zat," the Troll woman said. "I've done it wiz stones and bones and poisonous berries. Why not wiz glass?"

There is a rumour in Londra, about a Christmas soup that is served at the Fuentes' Soup Kitchen, near the river. People whisper that those who eat it cry golden tears afterwards. They also say that the soup is not served to everyone and that two young women — one with long, red hair and one with only one hand — decide who gets a bowl.

There are many stories told in Londra. And not all of them are true.

But I believe this one is.

Cornelia Funke is the highly acclaimed, award-winning and bestselling author of the *Inkheart* trilogy, *Dragon Rider*, *The Thief Lord* and the *Reckless* series, which is published by Pushkin Press. Born in 1958 in the German town of Dorsten, she worked as a social worker for a few years before turning first to illustration and then to writing. Her books have now sold more than 20 million copies worldwide and have been translated into 37 languages. Cornelia lives in Los Angeles.

We created Pushkin Children's Books to share tales from different languages and cultures with younger readers, and to open the door to the wide, colourful worlds these stories offer.

From picture books and adventure stories to fairy tales and classics, and from fifty-year-old bestsellers to current huge successes abroad, the books on the Pushkin Children's list reflect the very best stories from around the world, for our most discerning readers of all: children.